Start Your Engines

By Ace Landers
Illustrated by Dave White

SCHOLASTIC INC.

New York Toronto London Auckland Sydney
Mexico City New Delhi Hong Kong Buenos Aires

ISBN-10: 0-545-02017-4
ISBN-13: 978-0-545-02017-6

24 23 22   13 14/0

Printed in the U.S.A.   40
First printing, September 2007

Today is race day.
The cars are on the track.

The cars start their engines.
The engines roar. It sounds
like thunder.

The cars circle the track slowly. The green flag waves. It is time to race.

The cars go fast.

The tires screech around the first turn.

These are some of the
fastest cars in the world.

Some cars go faster
than 200 miles per hour.

The cars race around the track.

The track is big.

The cars try to
pass each other.

The red car moves to the
outside of the track.

The blue car moves to
the inside.

The drivers use skill to change lanes at high speed.

The blue car drives
past the red car!

Each car wants to
be in the lead.

The first car to cross
the finish line will win.

Some cars drive too fast.

This car is moving faster
than 200 miles per hour.

Oh, no! The orange car
spins out. It has a flat tire.

It is time for a pit stop.

In the pit, cars get
new tires and more gas.

The orange car is back in the race!

The cars speed to
the finish line.

The cars are driving
at top speed.

The checkered flag waves above the finish line.

Who won the race?

It is a close finish.

We have a winner!